FERRIS FLEET THE WHEELCHAIR WIZARD

by Annie Dalton
illustrated
by Carl Pearce

Tamarind

To Sophie and Izzie with love
A.D.
For Em & my cousins,
who won't let me grow up
C.P.

Published by Tamarind Ltd, 2005
PO Box 52
Northwood
Middx HA6 1UN

Edited by Simona Sideri

ISBN 978 1 870 51673 0

Printed in Singapore

Chapter 1
The Smallest Greenest World

The first time my mum left me, to go on a secret mission for the Cosmic Peace Police (CPP), I was only six months old. She swears she could hear my screams all the way to the star-port.

When I was older, Mum explained why her work took her away so much.

"I'd love to stay home, Oscar," she would sigh, packing her overnight bag. "But I have to show these people how to get along, instead of starting wars."

I was proud my mum had such an important job. As time went by, I got used to her zipping off to a different planet every few weeks. The same way I got used to her late night phone calls from weird star systems no-one had ever heard of.

I got used to it. But I never liked it.

CPP baby-sitters all look the same, with their sharp suits and blank faces. It's useless cracking a joke. They don't know how to smile. Anyway, they never hear a thing you tell them.

Too busy talking into their phones. As for their cooking! You can get tired of take-away pizza, you know.

I never told Mum how I felt. She had enough to cope with, being a cosmic troubleshooter and bringing up a kid.

But she must have guessed, because after my baby sister Ruby was born, Mum said she was tired of whizzing through space, fixing people's troubles. "I keep dreaming that I live in this quiet, green little world," she said. "In my dream, all I do is grow vegetables and spend time with my beautiful children."

So she handed in her notice and went searching for the smallest, greenest world she could find.

One night, the phone rang beside my bed. "Can't talk long, Oscar," Mum yelled, through the bleeps and crackles of deepest space. "I've found this incredibly cheap house on World Nine, between the mountains and the bay. It's my dream come true."

"Grab it, quick!" I bellowed back. "Hurray!" I whispered to my little sister. "No more CPP baby-sitters. Ever."

I fell in love with our new home the minute we arrived. World Nine is warm and wild and there are hardly any cars, and on summer nights the air smells as sweet and spicy as pumpkin pie.

A few days after we moved in a neighbour dropped by. "My name's Miss Coralie Creek, but you can call me Coralie," she said.

I think Miss Creek was lonely. She talked more and ate faster than anyone I ever saw. And somehow, by the time she was on her fifth slice of Mum's homemade cake, she got on to wizards.

It turned out that World Nine is full of them. In fact our nearest town, Lonelyheart, has its own wizards' university!

Mum didn't know whether to laugh or to cry. "You mean I've brought my children to the other end of the universe, so some cranky old wizard can turn them into frog spawn?" she wailed.

"Most wizards in Lonelyheart are harmless," Miss Creek explained. Then she lowered her voice. "The only one to watch out for is Marshbone. He's the most cold-hearted creature that ever drew breath."

She glanced nervously at the darkening sky and said she had better hurry home. Then she jumped on her bike and rode off so fast, I'm surprised her pedals didn't catch fire.

I looked up at the mountain. For the first time I noticed a strange tower hidden in the clouds. Purple lightning flickered around it.

"That's what scared Miss Creek," I thought.

When I told Mum what I suspected, she sighed and ruffled my hair. "Never mind Oscar. Our new life together is worth a wizard or two!"

But that night she locked all the doors and the windows. The next day I noticed she kept tight hold of me and Ruby when we went into town.

I'd never lived on a magic world before. I couldn't tell who were the wizards and who were just ordinary World Niners. I was extra polite to everyone, just in case.

Weeks passed and nothing happened. Unless you count Mum getting started on her vegetable patch.

Then early one morning, a CPP starship landed outside the house. Two worried-looking men in suits got out. One of them was Mum's old boss.

"I can't believe these people! Bothering me in the middle of breakfast," Mum grumbled. But she hurried out to meet them with my sister in her arms.

A minute later she was back. "Oscar, would you bring us some iced tea?" She seemed worried and dashed straight back out.

I couldn't hear what the men were saying, but it seemed like they were trying to convince Mum of something.

She wasn't agreeing, whatever it was.

When I brought the tea out, my mother said sharply, "Our guests are starving, Oscar. Will you bring some cake, too?"

After I took out the cake tin, things went quiet, until Mum yelled for me to take Ruby for her nap.

I tried to hear what the men were saying, as I tucked my sister into her crib, but their voices were too low. It had to be something serious, to bring the head of the Cosmic Peace Police to our lonely little corner of the galaxy.

At last, the starship took off in a burst of coloured lights. I found Mum pulling up thistles.

"Are you going away again?" I asked her.

"You know I've given up work," she replied. "My old boss just has a little problem he doesn't know how to deal with."

"Not true," I said. "Someone's starting a big war and the CPP want you to help stop it."

Mum pricked herself. "I told them to find someone else," she mumbled, sucking her bleeding finger.

"But everyone knows you're the best, Mum. If you don't go, who will?"

"I don't know. But I can't leave my babies, with some wicked wizard living at the bottom of my garden. And I hated those CPP baby-sitters as much as you did."

I knew Mum felt bad about letting her boss down. I didn't want her to go. But if she stayed home, there might be a war in space.

"What if I found a sitter," I said. "A good one. Would you go then?"

"No! Yes... I don't know..." wailed Mum. "It's impossible. The starship has to leave tomorrow night."

"That's heaps of time," I said. "We'll put up a notice at that university Miss Creek told us about."

Mum's eyebrows shot up. "The wizard university? That's like inviting the big bad wolf to sit for the three little pigs!"

"Miss Creek said the local wizards are harmless," I reminded her. "And students always need money."

So, when Ruby woke up, Mum drove us to the university and I put up a card on the student notice board. It started...

?
RETRO WORLD
DJ MCKELLN
SALE
TONES

**HAVE YOU
GOT WHAT IT TAKES
TO BE A HERO?
IF SO, PROVE IT.
BREAKFAST INCLUDED.**

Students are always hungry too.

Mum still wasn't sold on my wizard baby-sitter idea. "I want someone who can change Ruby's nappy without sticking pins into her," Mum objected. "Not some swaggering teenage wizard eating us out of house and home!"

"Trust me," I told her. "I know what I'm doing."

I did too. I knew we needed someone magic and brave. Someone who could keep one step ahead of Marshbone, in case of trouble. A **good** wizard, that's what I was looking for.

I heard a sweet humming sound. There was a flash of colour, like the wings of a bird of paradise. A wheelchair flew by so fast I couldn't see who was steering it. I just caught the words he was singing in a husky out-of-tune voice.

My worries instantly melted away. I grinned at Mum. "We'll find someone perfect. I know we will."

Mum smiled too, but she still looked worried. As we left, a student wizard spotted my card and started reading it aloud to his friends.

So far, so good. Now all we had to do was wait.

Chapter 2
Heroes, Wizards and Apple Slime

The wizards began arriving the next morning while it was still dark. I looked down from my bedroom window and saw an impatient crowd gathering.

"They're here, Mum!" I yelled and ran out to meet them.

"O.K., Shortstuff," yawned a wizard in dark glasses. "I'm your hero, so stop looking. Do I get a film contract, my picture in the papers, two week's supply of jelly beans? What's the deal?"

"The deal is, if you pass the tests, you get the job," I explained. But my heart sank. Show-off wannabe film star wizards weren't what I had in mind at all. Had I made a mistake?

"Is it very dangerous?" asked the smallest wizard eagerly. "Will it use every ounce of our skill?"

"I can't tell you, yet," I said, trying not to laugh. "But it's extremely well paid. Can I have your names for our records."

The wannabe film star wizard's name was Chancey. His

sidekick was a real smoothy called Ludo. The pair whispered to each other when they thought I couldn't see.

I heard Chancey hiss, "We showed him!" And Ludo cackled with glee behind his hand.

At last I asked, "Have I missed anyone?" But I hadn't.

Ludo rubbed his belly. "It said breakfast on that card."

I glanced hopefully down the mountain path. I listened hard. But there was no-one coming.

"*Not a star or a fish...*" I sang softly. Where had I heard that tune before?

"No-one will turn up now, Oscar," I told myself. So why did I feel as if I was still waiting? "Follow me," I sighed.

The wizards looked surprised to see a baby bath in the garden.

"Each of these tests was scientifically designed," I said. "Anyone refusing to do them must leave the contest immediately."

The sporty wizards started jogging on the spot, flexing their muscles. "Will we need, like, swords?" asked one.

Mum came out, set down two steaming jugs and rushed back indoors.

"Breakfast at last," gloated Ludo.

Mum came out again with my sister under her arm. "Wrong. Bath time," she said.

"We've got to b-bath a real b-baby?" stammered the smallest wizard.

"It's scientific, Peeble," hissed his friend. "If they say bath the kid, then bath the kid."

It's lucky me and Mum were there, or Ruby would never have come out of that bath alive!

But finally she was dry and dressed. Which is more than you can say for the wizards.

"Does she always scream this loud?" asked Peeble, blocking his ears.

"She wants her breakfast," I told him. "Ruby has cereal and apple sauce. The rest of us are having pancakes."

"You never said we had to *cook* the breakfast," complained Ludo.

"You never asked," I answered.

The wizards used zillions of matches, figuring out the cooker.

They swore they followed the instructions on Ruby's cereal packet. It still came out looking like cat sick.

And you wouldn't believe their apple sauce. It was more like apple slime.

Not one wizard knew how to make pancakes.

"Can we use magic?" asked Peeble nervously.

"You've got to eat it," Mum grinned.

The magic pancakes turned out very strange.

Peeble's flew away before he could put syrup on it.

When Ludo took a bite out of his pancake, it hissed like a snake and wriggled off into the grass.

At this point Mum decided breakfast was officially over.

All the wizards looked exhausted, and no-one had had a thing to eat.

"I wouldn't trust these fellows with my goldfish," whispered Mum. "I'm stopping this contest, before someone gets hurt."

"Wait, Mum!" I pleaded. "Someone else is going to come. I can feel it!"

"But who?" said Mum in despair. "And when?"

Then we both heard it. A high sweet humming sound.

Ludo heard it too. He swallowed.

"I told you those chains were rusty," hissed Chancey. "He's escaped!"

I ran to gaze down the mountain, my heart thumping.

The humming grew louder.

At each bend in the path I caught flashes of brilliant colour, like the wings of a bird of paradise.

The colours flashed faster and brighter. Suddenly, there he was.

"Sorry I took so long," said the handsome young wizard in the wheelchair. "Oh, my name's Ferris Fleet, but most people call me Fleet."

I couldn't speak. I just grinned.

I ran beside him all the way back to the others. "Mum, Mum, it's Fleet!" I shouted.

"You're too late!" snapped Ludo.

"Only because you chained him up underwater," Peeble's friend pointed out.

"Anyway Ruby needs another bath now, don't you?" crooned Peeble.

It was true. She was covered in apple slime.

"They've taken the bath away," said Chancey at once.

"Hmmn," said Fleet. "No bath, eh?" He took my slimy little sister in his arms. She gazed at him wide-eyed.

"Not a star or a fish," he sang softly. **"Not a bird or a wish..."**

Suddenly he spun his wheelchair round fast, leaving a brilliant tail of light like a comet's tail.

An elegant bath appeared on the grass. Sweet smelling steam rose from it.

"May I?" asked Fleet. He whisked off Ruby's babygro and gently lowered her into the water.

"Don't forget her hair," murmured Peeble. "Oops! No jug."

"I'll think of something," said Fleet.

The next minute a tiny baby elephant was solemnly spraying water all over Ruby. My sister laughed so much, I thought she was going to choke.

"That's so unhygienic," said Chancey jealously.

"Watch how you dry her," warned Peeble. "She's like an eel."

"Shut up, frog-face!" hissed Ludo. "You didn't help me."

"That's because I don't like you," explained Peeble calmly.

Fleet wrapped Ruby in a towel so soft, she looked as if she was peeping out of a cloud. When she came out, she was dressed from head to toe.

"Time for breakfast," said Peeble.

"Bacon and eggs," shouted someone.

"Cornmeal porridge," yelled someone else.

"Children first," said Fleet. He plucked a pretty china bowl from the air. It brimmed with creamy cereal. In the centre was a golden heart-shaped blob of perfect apple sauce. "That's Ruby's," he beamed. "Now Oscar's". A perfect pancake sailed through the air and landed on my plate.

"Mr Fleet," interrupted Mum crisply. "Do you know any jokes? Incredibly stupid ones? The kind that make small boys roll around in agony?" She was wearing her Cosmic Peace Police face. What was Mum up to?

"Hmmn," said Fleet thoughtfully. "Let me see." His eyes twinkled. "Knock, knock?"

"Who's there?" I yelled.

"Dwayne," grinned Fleet.

"Dwayne who?"

"Dwayne the bath quickly, I'm dwowning!"

It was the worse joke ever. I rolled on the grass in agony.

When I sat up again, Mum was telling Fleet he was the winner of the baby-sitting contest.

Those villains, Chancey and Ludo, were nowhere to be seen.

CHAPTER 3

KIDNAP!

The starship was waiting to take Mum away.

"Take care of my children, Fleet!" she said. But I knew Mum trusted Ferris Fleet to keep us safe while she was gone.

"Hope you stop the war, Mum!" I called.

Minutes later, her ship took off. I watched until I couldn't tell which was the ship and which were stars.

I heard Fleet say, "Could you go for spaghetti and meat balls, Oscar?"

We ate outside. The World Nine air smelled spicy as pumpkin pie. All the crickets in the neighbourhood were playing their tinny little sweet-sweet song.

"Fleet?" I said. "If they chained you up underwater, how did you escape?"

He smiled. "Wonderwheels saved me."

I stared at him. "Your wheelchair? You mean it's magic? But why did Ludo and Chancey want to stop you entering our contest?"

“Oh, that,” he said. “Their warped idea of fun. Still, forgive and forget, that’s my motto.”

I tipped my chair back and stared at the mountain. Marshbone’s tower was hidden in swirling clouds, which only made it spookier.

I thought about what Fleet had just said. Somehow, Chancey and Ludo did not strike me as the forgiving kind.

“Won’t they try to get their own back? Because you won our baby-sitter contest?”

Fleet shook his head. “They’re probably in The Merry Oyster right now, drowning their sorrows,” he grinned. “Forget them, Oscar. They’re pond scum.”

I waved my fork. “There! Forgotten that pond scum already.”

This reminded me of a joke. “Fleet, what kind of cola do frogs drink?”

“I don’t know. What kind?”

“Croakacola – nah nah nah-nah nah!”

Fleet spluttered into his spaghetti. “That’s terrible!”

“I know,” I said happily.

That night I woke from a bad dream to find my room full of unfriendly shadows. In my dream, Marshbone tried to kidnap us while Mum was away.

My sister woke up too and started to cry.

Before I could move, Fleet’s magic wheelchair came humming in. I couldn’t see it, but I felt its colours glowing in the dark.

Fleet took Ruby in his arms and sang.

"Not a star or a fish. Not a bird or a wish..."

"Fleet," I called sleepily, "What's that you keep singing? Is it a spell?"

"That would be telling," he said. I knew he was smiling.

"Is it a riddle, then?"

"It's a mystery, Oscar," he said softly. "That's what it is."

I fell asleep, still wondering.

It's funny. When Mum left me with those CPP sitters, the days crawled by like one big, long yawn. But I'm telling you, when you're with Ferris Fleet, things happen so fast you don't get time to blink.

I missed Mum and everything. But Fleet was the best sitter ever. He never got tired. And he had brilliant ideas.

Each time I thought of something to do, Fleet came up with something wilder.

When I suggested racing Wonderwheels on my mountain bike, Fleet said, "Think **BIG**, Oscar! How about a race track with real racing cars!"

And when I asked if we could build a tree house, Fleet said, "That sounds wonderful. But we can do better. Think **BIG!** Make it a tree castle!"

We both burst out laughing.

"A castle in the air!" we shouted at the exact same moment. I helped with hammering. Fleet only used magic on the really hard bits.

"The trick to magic is knowing when NOT to use it," he explained.

After the castle was ready, I said, “Let’s be knights, defending our castle from the enemy.”

Quick as lightning, Fleet said, “With a cannon that fires flour bombs and a slap-up banquet afterwards.”

The food fight was my idea. We got so messy, we needed a baby elephant *each* to get us clean. Finally, we were decent again and Ruby was tucked up in her crib, sucking her thumb.

“There’s a whole hour left before bedtime,” Fleet smiled. “What shall we do?”

“Fireworks!” I shouted. I waited for Fleet to top my idea with a wilder one, the way he always did. He’d do better than tiddly old sparklers, I knew he would.

Fleet seemed uneasy. “Indoor fireworks, you mean?”

“Of course not! Indoor fireworks are sad. Think **BIG**, you silly moose!” I teased him. “I mean **HUGE**, splendiferous, **COSMIC** fireworks, that can be seen from the other side of the galaxy!”

Fleet shook his head. “Not tonight, Oscar,” he said. “But I’ll teach you to juggle if you like?”

I got angry then. “Why are you so mean?” I yelled. “You tell me to think big, then you don’t like it when I do. I don’t want to learn to do stupid juggling! You’re a horrible pig and I’m going to bed.” I stormed off to my room.

But I felt ashamed. I shouldn’t have yelled like that.

A few minutes later, I heard a familiar humming outside my room. I ran to open the door.

The hall was empty. "Fleet?" I said anxiously. "Where are you?"

"Waiting for you," called Fleet's voice. "Hurry up!"

He must be on the verandah. What was that wizard up to? I opened the door and stepped out into the night. "Fleet?"

There was a sound like soft rain. Showers of light fizzed down from the roof. Then... **WHUMF!**

The air exploded with teeny rockets the size of jelly beans.

"Fireworks!" I breathed. "Doll's-house sized fireworks."

The display was cosmic. Completely splendiferous. I clapped and cheered. I wanted it to go on for ever. But one by one the tiny fireworks spun off into the night.

Words appeared, like floating candles in the dark.

I gasped. "Wonderwheels did that?"

"Of course," said Fleet. And there he was, beaming. "Friends?" he said.

I hugged him. "Friends!"

But I noticed that Fleet was looking around uneasily.

"Is something wrong?" I asked.

"I thought I heard something."

"Probably a firework burning out. Fleet, I didn't know Wonderwheels was so cool. What else can she do? I'm not a bit tired." I gabbled.

"Sorry, Oscar. It's bedtime," said Fleet firmly. "I'll just make sure your sister slept through those whizz-bangs."

I had forgotten all about Ruby.

I tiptoed into our room and pulled off my clothes. "Not a sound," I said. "She's sleeping like a baby dormouse."

But Fleet who came in behind me cried, "No!" and switched on the lamp.

The hairs stood up on my neck.

Ruby's crib was empty.

Chapter 4
Wonderwheels to the Rescue

"**Its my fault** for having a tantrum about the fireworks," I shivered.

"No, it's mine," said Fleet. "I forgot to be careful."

"They were only teeny fireworks. Marshbone couldn't have seen them."

Fleet shook his head. "Marshbone didn't take Ruby. He gets other wizards to do his dirty work."

"I bet I know which wizards, too," I said angrily. "I knew Chancey and Ludo would try to get their revenge."

Fleet was thinking hard. "There are hundreds of paths up that mountain. If we want to save your sister, we have to be the first to reach Marshbone's tower."

"You mean, we're going to go and get her back?" My heart was thumping.

"Hop on," ordered Fleet. "There's no time to lose."

I felt worried about Ruby, but I was excited too. Instead of being sent to bed, I was going on an adventure.

"Hold on tight," said Fleet. And he started to sing, "Not a star or a fish. Not a bird or a wish..."

Wonderwheels went zooming off into the darkness, like a comet. We flew so fast, the wind snatched my breath away.

"Keep your elbows in," yelled Fleet. "And don't look down!"

But I did, and gasped.

On one side of the wheelchair, there was only the rush of empty space. Up and up we climbed, skimming round terrifying bends and under waterfalls. It was like the scariest helter-skelter ever invented.

"Be brave, Ruby," I whispered. "We're coming to save you!"

Then my hair stood on end. Was Wonderwheels crazy? We were heading for solid rock!

Just as I was sure we'd crash, we swooped through an invisible opening.

We were actually inside the mountain, hurtling through the dark. Wonderwheels lit up at once with a helpful glow.

Mountains don't smell so great inside, unless you adore mouldy mushrooms. Moths flitted amongst pale plants and spooky pools. A bat flapped out of nowhere.

"Leave me alone, you creepy thing!" I told it.

Then I was gulping night air and we were outside again, careering up the mountain under the stars.

Suddenly I felt claws stick into me.

"AAArgggh! A bat!" I shrieked. "Leave me alone!"

Fleet couldn't stop laughing. "It's not a bat. It's a baby owl," he explained. "And it looks very surprised."

I touched cool feathers, puffy as dandelion fluff. I felt a tiny skittery heartbeat.

"Sorry if I scared you," I whispered. I didn't mind its claws, now I knew it was an owl, not a bat.

"Hold tight!" shouted Fleet. I frantically leaned to one side as we skidded round a sharp bend on two wheels. "And this," yelled Fleet, "is where Marshbone might turn nasty,"

WHUMF!

The sky tore like an old sheet. A sizzle of lightning zapped the ground behind us.

WHUMF!

This time the lightning struck in front.

"He must have seen us coming!" I screamed.

"Marshbone sees everything," Fleet shouted in my ear.

WHUMF! WHUMF! WHUMF!

Lightning hurtled from all directions.

Flames sprang up all around us. There was so much magic in the air, I could smell it. Heavy and sweet like a field of lilies.

"Will Wonderwheels be okay?" I bellowed.

"She's in wheelchair heaven," Fleet bellowed back. "Adventures keep her young."

Suddenly the storm fizzled out.

Wonderwheels braked hard. A tower rose up ahead of us.

It was the colour of marshes in the moonlight. An open door banged on its hinges.

To my horror, Wonderwheels went humming right into Marshbone's lair.

"ARE YOU CRAZY?" my voice boomed round the silent tower. I didn't mean to shout.

But somebody heard me. A long bony somebody, crouching on the stairs.

"Keep the noise down, boy," he pleaded. "Those spells have completely worn me out!"

I was shocked. This wizard looked wicked all right! I was so busy staring at Marshbone that I was startled when he spoke.

"Is that a real owl, Oscar?" he asked.

I nodded.

"You should always wear one. It suits you." And Marshbone laughed, like a little kid.

We've got it all wrong, I thought. Marshbone's not a monster. He'd never hurt Ruby. Then I saw his eyes. They were as empty as moons.

"I'll look after your sister really well," he said hungrily. "She'll be better off with me. I'd never go away and leave her with a sitter."

"What?" I said. I couldn't believe my ears.

"I've got her the sweetest crib. Would you like to see it?"

I didn't answer. I was too busy working out why Marshbone's tower felt so creepy.

There were no scary cobwebs or cauldrons or dusty spell books. Everything was beautiful. Soft rugs, beautiful furniture… It was perfect. Too perfect.

I imagined my sister knocking over ornaments and dribbling apple sauce. He thinks she's like a baby in a catalogue, I thought. He's got no idea.

A cry floated through the air. The kind babies make when they're really scared.

I heard Ludo and Chancey squabbling outside the tower. "You take her!"

"I'm not touching her. She's wet and smelly."

"Hold tight," Fleet whispered in my ear. With a screech of tyres, Wonderwheels zoomed to the rescue.

Ludo and Chancey weren't expecting to see a magic wheelchair racing straight at them!

I grabbed my sister easily. Then Wonderwheels swerved and we whizzed on past.

"Hush, hush," I murmured into Ruby's hair. "I'm here now."

Marshbone stumbled after us. "Don't take her away," he wailed. "I need her."

"Then get a puppy," I yelled. "Ruby's not a pet, she's a person. Can you change her nappy when she's messy? Can you sing when she gets scared?"

Marshbone looked horrified. "Messy?" he repeated. "Scared? Why would she be scared? I'll be here, to love her for ever and ever."

"Maybe you *see* everything, Marshbone. But you don't understand ANYTHING." I sighed.

Now we'd got Ruby back safe and sound, I felt sorry for this strange lonely wizard. Grown ups frighten him, I thought. That's why he wanted a harmless little baby to love.

"Look," I said. "Drop in when Mum's back. You could have tea and cake. Think about it."

"Tea with your mother?" said Marshbone. "How sweet!" He looked panic stricken. "Actually, I'm rather out of practice with people."

"What are we, then?" demanded Ludo. "Aren't we people?"

No, you're pond scum, I thought. "Think about it, Marshbone," I repeated. "But only when Mum's home," I quickly added.

The sun was rising as we reached our front gate.

We whizzed past Mum's vegetable patch and I saw tiny, emerald green pumpkin seedlings peeping through the dirt. I remember how Mum first saw this little green world in her dreams.

Now, thanks to Ferris Fleet, we could live here safely for ever.

When we reached my room, the owl fluttered to my pillow. "Welcome home, Nesbit," I yawned, falling into my bed.

"You're calling that owl Nesbit?" asked Fleet.

"Yes, because he's so small and sweet."

My eyes closed. I wasn't asleep. I still saw flashing

colours, like a bird of paradise. I still heard Fleet singing.

"Not a star or a fish. Not a bird or a wish..."

Maybe Fleet thought I was sleeping, because for the first time he finished the song that was also a magic riddle.

Then he leaned over my bed and whispered the answer. "It's Wonderwheels, you silly moose!"

Even with my eyes shut I knew he was smiling.

With a mystery solved, my sister safe in her crib and a baby owl to watch over us, I started feeling deliciously drowsy.

I vaguely heard a starship land in the garden. I think I even heard Mum come in to check on me. But don't ask me what she and Ferris Fleet said to each other. Because by then I was fast asleep.

OTHER TAMARIND TITLES

TAMARIND READERS:
The Day Ravi Smiled - NEW
Hurricane

BLACK PROFILE SERIES:
Benjamin Zephaniah
Lord Taylor of Warwick
Dr Samantha Tross
Malorie Blackman
Jim Brathwaite
Baroness Patricia Scotland of Asthal
Chinwe Roy

The Life of Stephen Lawrence

AND FOR YOUNGER READERS
A Safe Place - NEW
Princess Katrina and the Hair Charmer
The Feather
The Bush
Boots for a Bridesmaid
Dizzy's Walk
Zia the Orchestra
Mum's Late
Rainbow House
Starlight
Marty Monster
Jessica
Yohance and the Dinosaurs
Kofi and the Butterflies